Sheetal tai

W9-DEX-877

This book belongs
to Arthav Karmik

For Emilia
A. McA.
To my brother in law Jeremy Wernert
T. M.

First published in 2007 in Great Britain by Gullane Children's Books,
an imprint of Pinwheel Limited, Winchester House, 259-269 Old Marylebone Road, London NW1 5XJ
Text copyright © 2007 by Angela McAllister
Illustrations copyright © 2007 by Tina Macnaughton

This 2007 edition published by Backpack Books by arrangement with Pinwheel Ltd.

ISBN-13: 978-0-7607-9174-5
ISBN-10: 0-7607-9174-0

Printed and bound in China

1 3 5 7 9 10 8 6 4 2

Little Fawn

Angela McAllister · Tina Macnaughton

BACK PACK BOOKS

The other fawns loved to chase and hide but there
was one meadow where they would never stray . . .

it was the home of great **Four Prongs.**

No one had ever seen Four Prongs. They had
only seen his huge shadow. Sometimes he stretched
out his long horns. Sometimes he crouched small.
All the young deer were afraid of him. Little Fawn
wouldn't even dare peep through the trees.

Day by day, the other fawns grew bold.
"Who will be the first to taste the grass in
Four Prong's meadow?" they said.
"I will," boasted one.
"Not before me," cried his brother.

Nobody asked shy Little Fawn.

"I wish I was brave, Mama," Little Fawn whispered that night.
"But you are," said her mother sleepily.
"Who, me?"

"Yes," her mother smiled. "I know you are still frightened of the wood, but you follow us every day, even though you are afraid. And that is very brave indeed." She licked Little Fawn's ears.
"You can do whatever you want to do."

Little Fawn lay awake watching the stars.
Could she really do whatever she wished?

Before dawn, Little Fawn crept silently out of the den and set off through the wood alone. Owls hooted. Night creatures scuttered through the leaves. The stream was icy cold.

Little Fawn trembled.

She sniffed.

She listened.

But she went bravely on.

When she reached the meadow of Four Prongs, she peered
between the trees. The moon shone down but nothing stirred.
Little Fawn took a step inside. She sniffed. She listened.

The meadow was empty.
"Oh," she sighed, "he's gone!"
Sleepy and disappointed, she lay
down alone and fell fast asleep.

Little Fawn woke up feeling very hungry, and she began to eat.
The grass was so good she hardly noticed the sun rise. Suddenly
she heard frightened cries from the edge of the meadow.
Everyone had been searching for her.

"Little Fawn! Watch out behind you!"

Little Fawn turned . . .
A dark shape lay long in the grass, stretching out towards her.
"Run," the young deer cried. "Run, Little Fawn, run!"

But Little Fawn didn't run. She
saw what they couldn't see . . .

On the hill stood a windmill, stretching its four arms in the morning
sun. With a creak the sails began to turn and below, its great shadow
stirred too. The other fawns stepped nervously into the meadow.
They laughed when they saw their mistake.
"You are the bravest, Little Fawn!" they agreed.

Little Fawn's mother led them all into the sun.
"Run and play now," she said proudly.
And brave Little Fawn sniffed the new morning,
smiled happily, and joined in the game.